# REAL WORLD MATH

# DINOSAUR dig

### Wendy Clemson and Frances Clemson

Tick Tock

An Hachette UK Company
www.hachette.co.uk
First published in the USA in 2013 by
TickTock, an imprint of Octopus Publishing Group Ltd
Endeavour House,189 Shaftesbury Avenue, London WC2H 8JY
www.octopusbooks.co.uk
www.octopusbooksusa.com

Copyright © Octopus Publishing Group Ltd 2013

Distributed in the US by
Hachette Book Group USA
237 Park Avenue, New York NY 10017, USA

Distributed in Canada by
Canadian Manda Group
165 Dufferin Street, Toronto, Ontario, Canada M6K 3H6

ISBN 978 1 84898 939 9

Printed and bound in China

10 9 8 7 6 5 4 3 2 1

Picture credits
t=top, b=bottom, c=center, l-left, r=right, f=far
1, 2, 3FR, 26B, 27T, 31T Lisa Alderson. 3FL, 3L, 3C, 3R, 6L, 6R, 17, 14BCL, 14BFR, 14BCR, 34T, 26T, 29B, 31B, 32 Simon Mendez.
5, 6C, 7B, 8L, 11B, 21, 23, 29T, 30 Luis Rey. 4TL, 4BL, 4TR, 8-9, 9T, 15B, 20, 27CL, 27C, 28T, 28L Shutterstock. 4BR BananaStock/Alamy.
14T David R. Frazier Photolibrary, Inc./Alamy. 19 Louie Psihoyos/Corbis. 15T Royalty-Free/Corbis. 24B, 25 The Natural History Museum, London. 27B Roger
Harris/Science Photo Library. 18 Larry Miller/Science Photo Library. 13 Sinclair Stammers/Science Photo Library.
7T, 10, 11T, 12T, 12B, 14BFL  27CR, 28FL, 28R, 28FR Ticktock Media Archive.
Front cover: Shutterstock
Back cover: Ticktock Media Archive

Every effort has been made to trace the copyright holders, and we apologize in advance for any unintentional omissions.
We would be pleased to insert the appropriate acknowledgement in any subsequent edition of this publication.

# Contents

Let's Start Digging....................4

Walking with Dinosaurs ...........6

Whose Footprint? .................8

Bony Clues .......................10

Fossil Finds .....................12

To the Museum ...................14

Labelling Finds...................16

Checking the Fossil Footprint...18

A New Display ....................20

Flying Visit.........................22

Dinosaur Parents .................24

Is this a Record? .................26

In the Shop........................28

Tips and Help .....................30

Answers ..........................32

**MATH SKILLS COVERED
IN THIS BOOK:**

**Numbers and the number system**
Comparing and ordering: p. 10
Comparing numbers: p. 6
Skip-counting by tens: p. 15
Skip-counting by twos: p. 7
Fractions: pp. 9–10, 23
Money: pp. 28–29
Number line: p. 24
Number order: p. 14
Odds and evens: p. 17

**Mental calculations**
Addition and subtraction: pp. 6, 8–9, 21–22, 29
Counting: pp. 6, 11, 20
Difference: p 22
Division: pp. 20, 26
Missing numbers: p. 24
Multiplication: pp. 9, 12, 15, 18, 20, 22

**Shape, space, and measurements**
Angles: p. 23
Comparing measures: pp. 12, 23–24, 26
Estimates: pp. 7, 13
Measures: pp. 8–12
Measuring equipment: p. 16
Measuring with a ruler: p. 11
Putting measures in order: p. 14
Scales and dials: p. 22
Solid shapes: p. 28
Units of measurement: pp. 7, 23
Using a ruler: p. 11

**Organizing data**
Bar graph: p. 13
Charts: pp. 11, 16, 18, 20
Grid maps: p. 9
Sorting: pp. 17, 19

**Problem solving**
Finding the difference: p. 22
Length: p. 10
Predicting patterns: p. 16
Figuring out costs: p. 29

**Supports math standards
for grades 2–4**

# Let's Start Digging

You have an exciting job. You're a dinosaur expert! Dinosaurs lived millions of years ago. You try to find their bones, eggs, and footprints. You use these clues to help you discover how dinosaurs lived. Then you tell everybody else what you have discovered!

## What does a dinosaur expert do?

Look for bones that have been buried for millions of years.

Write about your finds and read what other scientists have written.

Display your dinosaur discoveries in a museum.

Sometimes you talk to children about your job.

**But did you know that dinosaur experts sometimes have to use math?**

In this book you will find lots of number puzzles that dinosaur experts have to solve every day. You will also get the chance to answer lots of number questions about bones and fossils and find out a lot about dinosaurs, too.

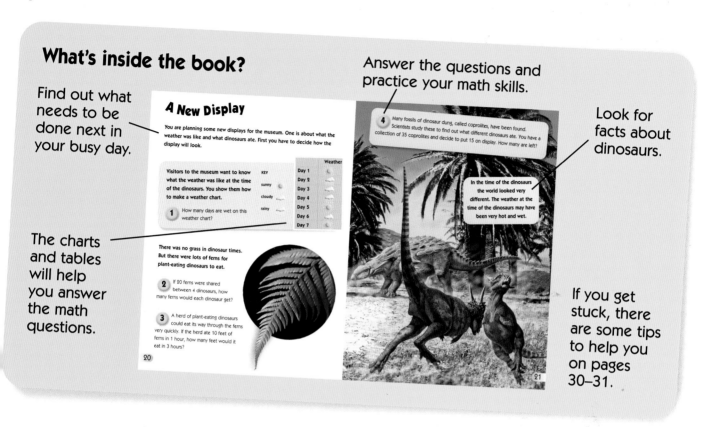

**What's inside the book?**

Find out what needs to be done next in your busy day.

The charts and tables will help you answer the math questions.

Answer the questions and practice your math skills.

Look for facts about dinosaurs.

If you get stuck, there are some tips to help you on pages 30–31.

**A New Display**

You are planning some new displays for the museum. One is about what the weather was like and what dinosaurs ate. First you have to decide how the display will look.

Visitors to the museum want to know what the weather was like at the time of the dinosaurs. You show them how to make a weather chart.

KEY
sunny
cloudy
rainy

Weather
Day 1
Day 2
Day 3
Day 4
Day 5
Day 6
Day 7

**1** How many days are wet on this weather chart?

There was no grass in dinosaur times. But there were lots of ferns for plant-eating dinosaurs to eat.

**2** If 20 ferns were shared between 4 dinosaurs, how many ferns would each dinosaur get?

**3** A herd of plant-eating dinosaurs could eat its way through the ferns very quickly. If the herd ate 10 feet of ferns in 1 hour, how many feet would it eat in 3 hours?

20

**4** Many fossils of dinosaur dung, called coprolites, have been found. Scientists study these to find out what different dinosaurs ate. You have a collection of 35 coprolites and decide to put 15 on display. How many are left?

In the time of the dinosaurs the world looked very different. The weather at the time of the dinosaurs may have been very hot and wet.

21

Are you ready to be a dinosaur hunter for the day?

You will need paper, a pencil, and a ruler, and don't forget to bring your shovel! Let's go...

# Walking with Dinosaurs

Hunting dinosaurs is not as difficult as you might think. Dinosaurs roamed the Earth millions of years ago. They have left a lot behind them, including footprints, eggs, and bones. Today you are going on a journey to search for dinosaur bones in North America.

The time when dinosaurs lived is divided into three different periods.

- **Cretaceous Period**
- **Jurassic Period**
- **Triassic Period**

This map shows some places where dinosaur fossils have been found.

Map of Canada and the United States

**1** How many Triassic sites are there?

**2** Which period has the most sites?

Here are some dinosaurs that lived in the different periods.

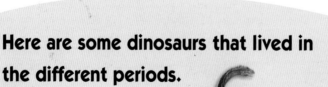

*Diplodocus*
lived 150 million years ago.

*Liliensternus*
lived 220 million years ago.

*Triceratops*
lived 70 million years ago.

**3** Which dinosaur lived longest ago?

You have arrived at a site in the desert where the ground is dry and rocky. You know dinosaurs used to live here. Suddenly you see a giant footprint.

**4** Look at this dinosaur footprint next to a hand. How many hands do you think might fit across this footprint?

**1     2 to 3     more than 3**

Some dinosaurs went around in groups called herds. This helped to protect them from enemies. A herd may have been very large. Fossil hunters have found up to 30 dinosaur skeletons in one place.

**5** Try making 30 by adding the same number many times. 30 is...
**30 ones          3 tens          how many twos?**

*Amargasaurus* may have travelled in herds. This dinosaur was 30 feet long, with two rows of spines down its neck.

# Whose Footprint?

You have to find out which dinosaur made this footprint. You look it up in a book. It looks like the footprint of *Iguanodon*. This dinosaur usually moved on all four feet but it could also stand on just its back feet. This made *Iguanodon* different from other dinosaurs.

**1** *Iguanodon* had three toes on each of its feet. Its front feet also had a thumb and a spike for holding plants. How many toes did *Iguanodon* have altogether?

**2** *Iguanodon* was 33 feet long from the tip of its nose to the end of its tail. If its tail was 10 feet long, how long was the rest of it?

A dinosaur footprint, showing the three toes of the back foot.

**You find three more footprints, and you decide to make some plaster casts to take back to the museum.**

**Instructions**

1. Mix the plaster with some water.
   Use 1 cup of water for 1 pack of plaster.
2. Pour the mixture into the footprint.
3. Wait 5 minutes for the plaster to dry.
4. Ease out the plaster cast.

**3** It takes you 15 minutes to make each plaster cast. How much of this time is spent waiting for the plaster to dry?

$\frac{1}{2}$  $\frac{1}{4}$  $\frac{1}{3}$

**4** How many cups of water do you need if you use 3 packs of plaster?

**5** If you make 8 plaster casts of each front foot and 3 casts of each back foot, how many casts will you have in all?

**6** Now you draw a plan to show where you found each footprint. Starting from the back left footprint, which footprint did you find 2 squares up and 2 squares to the right?

front right

front left

back right

back left

# Bony Clues

You collect other bits of bone that you find. Then you spot something half-buried in the sand. You hurry towards it, careful not to tread on any other fossils. It looks as if it might be part of the leg of the dinosaur *Stegosaurus*.

*Stegosaurus* was 30 feet long. It had two rows of plates along its back. At the end of its tail it had 4 long, sharp spikes that it could swing at attackers.

**1** One of the bits of bone you find is 10 inches long. If this is half of the bone, how long was the bone?

## LENGTH OF BONES

You collect three dinosaur bones. You draw a sketch of them and write the length of the bone underneath.

Front leg bone
3 feet

Hip bone
7 feet

Back leg bone
10 inches

**2** Put the bones in order from longest to shortest.

Now you have found a tooth – this is very exciting. We know what dinosaurs ate by what their teeth look like. Plant-eaters' teeth were not very sharp. Meat-eaters had very sharp teeth. They were pointed and of different sizes.

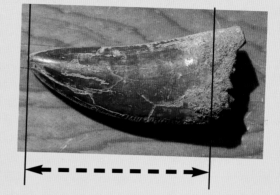

**3** Measure this dinosaur tooth with a ruler. What is its length?

You check a chart that tells you which kinds of dinosaurs were meat-eaters and which were plant-eaters.

**4** How many dinosaurs in this chart are plant-eaters?

**5** How many dinosaurs are there altogether?

| Plant-eaters | Meat-eaters |
|---|---|
| *Diplodocus* | *Tyrannosaurus* |
| *Stegosaurus* | *Oviraptor* |
| *Triceratops* | *Velociraptor* |
| *Iguanodon* | |

*Tyrannosaurus* weighed about 6 tons. That's the same as more than 200 children!

# Fossil Finds

Next, you visit some cliffs. This is a good place to find some fossils of sea creatures. You are looking for ammonites, which were alive at the same time as the dinosaurs, and trilobites, which lived millions of years before them.

There were over 10,000 different types of trilobites. They varied in size from ¾ of an inch to 18 inches.

**1** Which of the numbers below mean 18 inches?

One and a half feet

1½ feet

A quarter of a foot

1 foot

Two feet

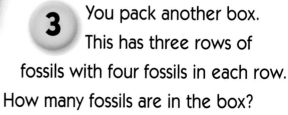
Trilobites were one of the first animals on Earth.

**2** You find three ammonite fossils like this. Each one is 10 inches across. You pack them side by side into a box. How wide does your box have to be?

**3** You pack another box. This has three rows of fossils with four fossils in each row. How many fossils are in the box?

**4** Look at this picture of a rock. How many ammonite fossils do you think are in this picture?

A. about 5

B. about 10

C. about 25

## COUNTING YOUR FINDS

**5** You find 4 plant fossils, 9 ammonites, and 6 trilobites. You draw a bar graph to show what you have found. But wait, you have made a mistake. Look at the graph. What's the mistake?

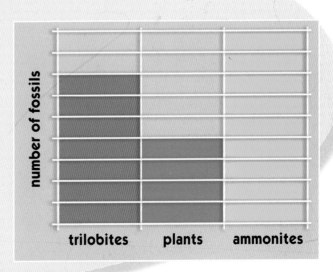

number of fossils

trilobites     plants     ammonites

# To the Museum

You now have to take your fossils back to the museum. Because you are on a site in the middle of the desert, you are picked up by helicopter and flown back to the museum.

The first thing you see at the museum is the awesome skeleton of the mighty *Tyrannosaurus*. This dinosaur moved around on its hind legs. It had between 50 and 60 teeth. It could easily crush the bones of other dinosaurs.

*Tyrannosaurus* had a huge head. Its skull was over 3 feet long.

**1** Which of these numbers are between 50 and 60?

**53   62   75   57   65   49**

*Tyrannosaurus* was big, but it was not the heaviest dinosaur. Many plant-eating dinosaurs weighed much more.

**Apatosaurus**
33 to 42 tons

**Triceratops**
7 to 13 tons

**Tyrannosaurus**
5 to 8 tons

**Brachiosaurus**
36 to 53 tons

**2** Put these in order from the lightest dinosaur to the heaviest dinosaur. Use the greatest weight for each kind of dinosaur.

One of your favorite exhibits at the museum is *Apatosaurus*. It took about 10 years for *Apatosaurus* to become fully grown. It may have lived for 100 years in all.

**3** How many tens are in 100?

*Apatosaurus* had a huge neck, which allowed it to feed on the leaves at the top of the tallest trees.

*Triceratops* was a plant-eater. Its name means "three-horned face." Its 3 horns helped it to defend itself against meat-eaters like *Tyrannosaurus*.

**4** There are 5 *Triceratops* on display. How many horns is that in all?

*Triceratops* lived in North America. It ate bushes and trees.

# Labelling Finds

You take your finds to the museum storeroom. Here you have to label each one. Each bone, tooth, fossil, or footprint is given a label with a code on it.

Row A | A2 | A4 | | A8

Row B | B3 | | B9 | B12

Row C | C10 | C15 | C20 |

**1** Which of these labels fill the gaps in the rows?

A1   C26   B8   B6   A6   C25

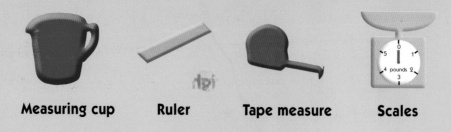

You also have to measure each of your finds.
Here are some of the measuring tools you use.

Measuring cup    Ruler    Tape measure    Scales

**2** Which tool would you use to measure:

**A** the length of a bone about the size of your hand?

**B** the weight of a fossil?

**C** the length of a hole dug to find fossils?

**D** water for making a plaster cast?

16

*Stegosaurus* might have used its plates to keep warm by facing them towards the sun.

You are now putting together a model of *Stegosaurus* for display. The plates to go on the model's back have been labelled. Each plate has been numbered so that it goes in the right place. One row is going to be odd numbers and one row even numbers.

**3** Sort the plates.
Which plates go in each row?

7  3  10  2  9  8  1  6  13  11  5  4  12  14

# Checking the Fossil Footprint

You unpack the plaster casts you made of the dinosaur footprints. Can you use them to learn more about the dinosaur that left them? You would like to know how tall it was and how fast it was moving.

**1** You can work out a dinosaur's height up to its hip using its footprint. You take the length of the dinosaur footprint and multiply it by 4. The footprints you found are 2 feet long. How high is your dinosaur, up to its hips?

**2** You now look at your dinosaur's stride length. This is the distance a dinosaur travels in two steps. Your dinosaur has steps that are 10 feet long. What is its stride length?

**3** With your dinosaur's hip height and stride length, you can work out how fast it was moving. Divide the length of stride by its hip height. This gives you a number. Look at this chart. Was your dinosaur running, trotting, or walking?

## DINOSAUR SPEED

| | stride length divided by hip height |
|---|---|
| walking | under 2 |
| trotting | between 2 and 3 |
| running | over 3 |

You now have to see if you can make a whole skeleton out of the bone fossils that you found.

**4** Put these bones in order, from the head of the dinosaur to its tail.

ribs

neck bone

front leg bones

skull

tailbones

Experts use tracks to learn about dinosaur behavior. One set of tracks means the dinosaur travelled alone. Sets of tracks that are side by side means the dinosaurs travelled in groups.

# A New Display

You are planning some new displays for the museum. One is about what the weather was like and what dinosaurs ate. First you have to decide how the display will look.

| | Weather |
|---|---|
| Day 1 | ☀ |
| Day 2 | 🌧 |
| Day 3 | ☁ |
| Day 4 | 🌧 |
| Day 5 | ☀ |
| Day 6 | ☁ |
| Day 7 | ☀ |

Visitors to the museum want to know what the weather was like at the time of the dinosaurs. You show them how to make a weather chart.

**KEY**

sunny ☀

cloudy ☁

rainy 🌧

**1** How many days are wet on this weather chart?

There was no grass in dinosaur times. But there were lots of ferns for plant-eating dinosaurs to eat.

**2** If 20 ferns were shared between 4 dinosaurs, how many ferns would each dinosaur get?

**3** A herd of plant-eating dinosaurs could eat its way through the ferns very quickly. If the herd ate 10 feet of ferns in 1 hour, how many feet would it eat in 3 hours?

**4** Many fossils of dinosaur dung, called coprolites, have been found. Scientists study these to find out what different dinosaurs ate. You have a collection of 35 coprolites and decide to put 15 on display. How many are left?

In the time of the dinosaurs the world looked very different. The weather at the time of the dinosaurs may have been very hot and wet.

# Flying Visit

One of your favorite subjects is creatures that could fly. *Archaeopteryx* is the oldest known bird. It had feathers and it could fly, although not very well. It was a very fierce hunter.

**1** What is the difference between *Archaeopteryx's* length and wingspan?

**2** *Archaeopteryx* had three claws on each wing. It used its claws to grasp onto branches. How many wing claws did it have in all?

**Here is a chart showing what *Archaeopteryx* measured.**

| ARCHAEOPTERYX | |
|---|---|
| Length | 12 inches |
| Wingspan | 20 inches |

**3** *Archaeopteryx* ate small animals and insects. How many insects are here?

**4** *Archaeopteryx* weighed between 12 and 24 ounces. If we put *Archaeopteryx* on a scale, which of these balances would be correct?

A

B

The biggest pterosaur had a wingspan of about 40 feet.

**During dinosaur times there were some reptiles that could fly. They were called pterosaurs.**

**5** Suppose this pterosaur makes a quarter-turn in a clockwise direction. Which picture shows the pterosaur after the turn?

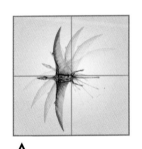

**A**

**B**

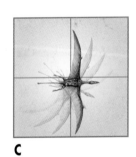

**C**

**6** Your star fossil is now going on display. It is a *Pterodactylus*. This flying reptile had a wingspan of 6 feet. Its body was half as long as its wingspan. Which is the correct display label?

### PTERODACTYLUS

**Habitat:** rivers and seas
**Wingspan:** 10 inches
**Body length:** 4 inches

Label A

### PTERODACTYLUS

**Habitat:** rivers and seas
**Wingspan:** 72 inches
**Body length:** 24 inches

Label B

### PTERODACTYLUS

**Habitat:** rivers and seas
**Wingspan:** 72 inches
**Body length:** 36 inches

Label C

# Dinosaur Parents

Dinosaurs laid eggs. You decide to create a display showing a dinosaur nest with some eggs.

The eggs of *Hypselosaurus* were laid in a row as the dinosaur walked along. These eggs are not in order. One is not here.

**1** Which one is missing?

2  8  12  4  6  10  9  13  1  3  7  5

Some dinosaur eggs were very big indeed. The eggs of *Hypselosaurus* were like soccer balls, at least 12 inches across.

**2** If you filled a *Hypselosaurus* egg with water, it could hold about four cups. How many ounces is that?

*Maiasaura* lived in groups. A group stayed near the eggs until the babies hatched. Each mother laid between 15 and 20 eggs.

**3** Which of these numbers are between 15 and 20?

17  12  25  52  10  16  19

**Some dinosaurs made nests and sat on their eggs to keep them warm, just like birds today. *Oviraptor* was one of these.**

**4** Look at these hatched dinosaur eggs.
Find the pieces that fit together to make whole eggs.

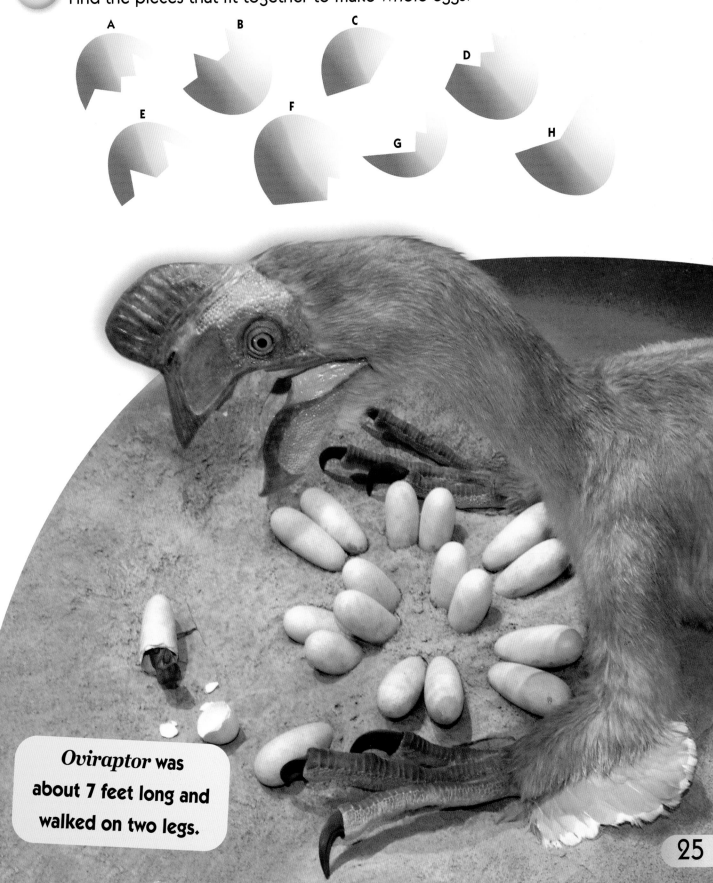

*Oviraptor* was about 7 feet long and walked on two legs.

# Is this a Record?

You have been asked to make a list of dinosaur record breakers. New dinosaur fossils are being found all the time, and so records have to be kept up-to-date.

## LONGEST

The longest dinosaurs were gigantic. They ate plants and they moved slowly. *Seismosaurus* was among the longest.

**1** *Seismosaurus* was 115 feet long. Do you think that is nearest the length of:
   **A)** a jump rope?    **B)** a bus?    **C)** 3 buses?

**2** Meat-eating dinosaurs were not so long, but one of the longest was *Tyrannosaurus*. It was 40 feet long. Do you think that is nearest the length of:
   **A)** a jump rope?    **B)** a bus?    **C)** 3 buses?

## TALLEST

The tallest dinosaurs, like *Brachiosaurus*, had long necks. They could reach up to eat the leaves at the top of tall trees.

**3** *Brachiosaurus* was about 80 feet tall. If you and your friends stood on each other's shoulders until you were as tall as *Brachiosaurus*, about how many children would there be?

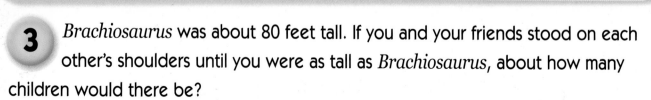

## 5,  25,  or 100?

## SMALLEST

One of the smallest dinosaurs was *Bambiraptor*. This dinosaur was only 3 feet long and weighed about 7 pounds.

**4** Which of these may weigh the same as *Bambiraptor*?

an egg

a shoe

a bag of potatoes

Some meat-eating dinosaurs were quite small. *Velociraptor* was about 7 feet long – and half of this length was its tail.

# In the Shop

All your displays are now ready for the Grand Opening tomorrow. On your way out of the museum, you go into the gift shop. You like the model insects inside see-through blocks.

The museum has some real insects from dinosaur times. The insects got trapped in sticky stuff called resin, which comes from trees. The resin became hard and turned into amber.

A          B          C

**1** Here are some plastic models of the amber. What are the names of these shapes?

**2** A plastic model costs $1.50. You give the cashier $2. How much change will you get?

A piece of amber showing insects that were trapped millions of years ago.

**3** Which of these fossils is the most expensive?

A          B          C          D

$3          75¢          $2.50          $3.75

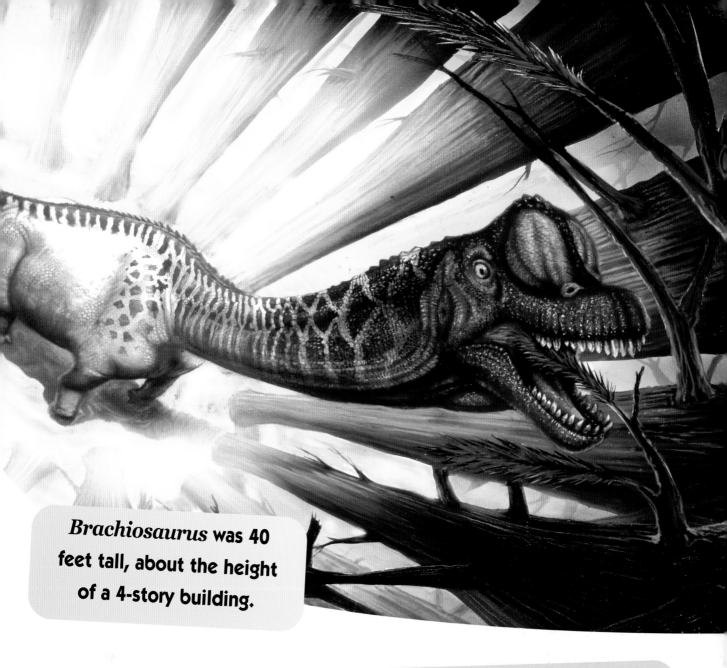

Brachiosaurus was 40 feet tall, about the height of a 4-story building.

**4** Look at the poster on the right. How much money do you save if you go on Grand Opening day?

**5** You bring two friends to the Grand Opening. How much will the entrance fee cost altogether?

**6** You love the exhibition! You go once for the Grand Opening and twice later. How much do you pay altogether?

## Meet *Allosaurus*
### and other dinosaurs!

Entrance fee.......................... $4

Entrance fee on
Grand Opening day............. $3

# Tips and Help

## PAGES 6–7

**Putting numbers in order** – To put these numbers of years in order, try looking at the hundreds first: 150 has one hundred, 220 has two hundreds, and 70 has no (zero) hundreds. In order, the longest ago is 220 million years, then 150 million years, and 70 million years is the most recent.

## PAGES 8–9

**Subtraction** – If we take away the length of *Iguanodon*'s tail from its total body length, we are doing a subtraction.

**Fractions** – A fraction is part of a whole. When we share or cut something into two equal parts, each part is the fraction ½ (one-half). If it is cut into three equal parts, each part is the fraction ⅓ (one-third), and in four equal parts, each would be ¼ (one-fourth).

## PAGES 10–11

**Putting measures in order** – Check that the measures are all made in the same unit of measurement. Here you can change them all to inches. Remember there are 12 inches in 1 foot.

**Measuring length** – To measure the length of something, be sure the zero, or left, edge of the ruler lines up with the end of the left-pointing arrow. The number where the right-pointing arrow ends is the lenght of the dinosaur tooth.

## PAGES 12–13

**Feet and inches** – There are 12 inches in 1 foot.

**Rows and columns** – 3 rows, each with 4 fossils, gives the same total as 4 rows, each with 3 fossils.

**Estimates** – When you say how many ammonites you think there are in the picture, this is an estimate. Careful estimates are useful when doing math.

## PAGES 14–15

**Numbers between** – To work out where numbers fit, think of a number line and order the numbers along it. Then you will see where they fit. Here your number line looks like this:

So only two numbers fit along your number line.

50  51  52  53  54  55  56  57  58  59  60

**Skip-count by 3s** – Skip-counting by 3s is the same as the numbers in the 3x table. It is good to remember them:
0 3 6 9 12 15 18 21 24 27 30 33 36

## PAGES 16–17

**Measuring tools** – It is important to choose the right measuring tool for a job. Remember that a cup is used to measure liquids, and scales are used to measure weight. A ruler and a tape measure are tools for measuring height, width, and length.

**Odds and evens** – Even numbers are the numbers in the counting pattern of twos: 2 4 6 8 10 12 14 16 18 20…. and so on. Odd numbers are the numbers not in this pattern; that is, 1 3 5 7 9 11 13 15 17 19…. and so on.

## PAGES 18–19

**Multiplying and dividing** – We can see how these are connected:
$2 \times 10 = 20$   and   $20 \div 10 = 2$

## PAGES 20–21

**Sharing** – Sharing is dividing a whole into equal parts. The whole is the total number of ferns. The number of ferns for each dinosaur is the same as the size of each share.

## PAGES 22–23

**Pounds and ounces** – 1 pound is 16 ounces.

**A ¼ turn** – There are four quarter-turns in one complete turn.

**Clockwise** – The direction in which the hands of a clock move.

clockwise

counterclockwise

## PAGES 24–25

**Cups and ounces** – 1 cup is 8 ounces.

## PAGES 26–27

**Longest, smallest, tallest** – Remember we say "longer," "smaller," or "taller" when we compare two things, and "longest," "smallest," and "tallest" when we compare three or more than three things. Here we are comparing lots of dinosaurs.

## PAGES 28–29

**Money** – One dollar is 100 cents.

# Answers

## PAGES 6–7

1  6
2  Cretaceous
3  *Liliensternus*
4  2 to 3
5  15 twos

## PAGES 8–9

1  12
2  23 feet
3  ⅓
4  3 cups
5  22 plaster casts
6  back right footprint

## PAGES 10–11

1  20 inches
2  hip bone, front leg bone, back leg bone
3  2 inches
4  4
5  7

## PAGES 12–13

1  one and a half feet and 1½ feet
2  30 inches
3  12
4  about 10 trilobites
5  graph shows 7 trilobites

## PAGES 14–15

1  53 and 57
2  *Tyrannosaurus*, *Triceratops*, *Apatosaurus*, and *Brachiosaurus*
3  10
4  15 horns

## PAGES 16–17

1  Row A - A6
   Row B - B6
   Row C - C25
2  A - ruler
   B - scales
   C - tape measure
3  D - measuring cup
   2, 4, 6, 8, 10, 12, and 14
   1, 3, 5, 7, 9, 11, and 13

## PAGES 18–19

1  8 feet
2  20 feet
3  trotting
4  skull, neck bone, front leg bone, ribs, tailbone

## PAGES 20–21

1  2 days
2  5 ferns
3  30 feet
4  20 coprolites

## PAGES 22–23

1  8 inches
2  6 claws
3  16 insects
4  B
5  C
6  Label C

## PAGES 24–25

1  11
2  32 ounces
3  16, 17, and 19
4  A and D
   B and E
   C and H
   F and G

## PAGES 26–27

1  C - 3 buses
2  B - 1 bus
3  25 children
4  bag of potatoes

## PAGES 28–29

1  A - sphere
   B - cube
   C - pyramid
2  50 cents
3  D
4  $1
5  $9
6  $11